ONE FINAL SHOT

A SHORT STORY

MICHAEL E. JONES

THAXTON PRESS

One Final Shot: A Short Story

ISBN 978-0-9890046-2-6 (ebook)

ISBN 979-8-9864354-1-1 (paperback)

www.mikejoneswrites.com

www.facebook.com/mikejoneswrites

www.twitter.com/mikejoneswrites

www.instagram.com/mikejoneswrites

mike@mikejoneswrites.com

Cover photo courtesy of U.S. Air Force

Published by Thaxton Press, LLC

thaxtonpress.com

sales@thaxtonpress.com

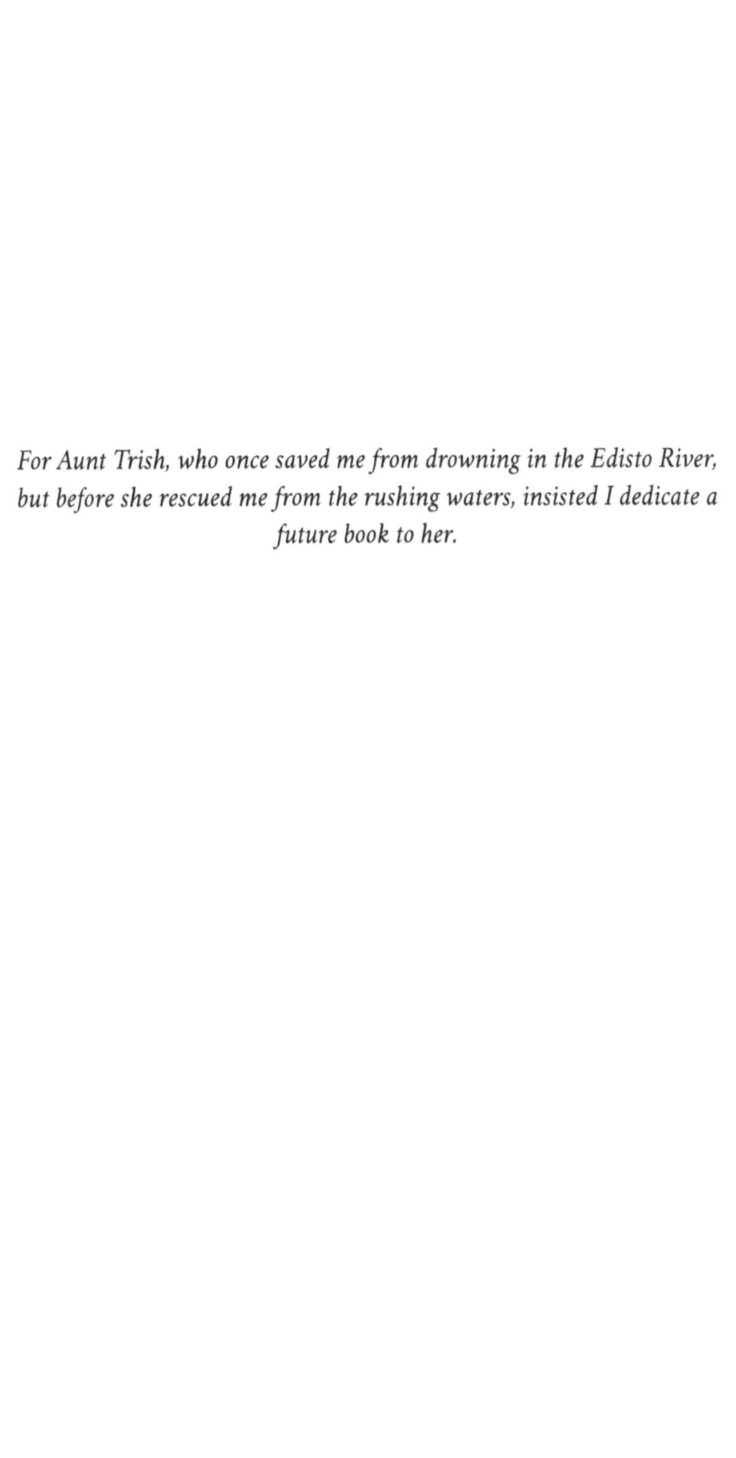

For Aunt Trish, who once saved me from drowning in the Edisto River, but before she rescued me from the rushing waters, insisted I dedicate a future book to her.

CONTENTS

1. One Final Shot   1
   Historical Note   32

Also by Michael E. Jones   33
About the Author   35
Acknowledgments   37

Sergeant Eddie Wheeler was the last American combat death of the Second World War. He was my father, and he was murdered by Hideo Wakita.

Murder. I guess people don't normally use that word to describe the act of killing in wartime. But I always considered Dad's death to be the outcome of a murderous deed. The war was already over when Wakita put a 20mm round right through my father's heart. As I watched my mama suffer through the years after Wakita killed Dad, I came to the realization that Wakita's lethal shot had ended my mother's life as well. She didn't die the day Wakita shot my dad, but she never truly lived afterward. I can't recall ever seeing a smile on her face, other than in a photo taken by my Dad the summer they were married. The woman I grew up with was not the same as the one in that photograph, and I held Hideo Wakita solely responsible for that.

I wish I could have known the person Mama had been before Wakita took Dad's life. Mama and Dad had been high school sweethearts, and in the summer of 1941, shortly after graduation, those two lovebirds got married. But it wasn't long before they had to put their married life on hold. Like most young men those days, Dad felt a need to serve his country, and he eventually enlisted in the US Army Air Forces.

The Army Air Forces sent Dad to train at different locations around the country and whenever she could, Mama would follow him. During the late Autumn of 1944, Dad was at Will Rogers field in Oklahoma City for photo-reconnaissance training. Mama figured they had chosen Dad for the reconnaissance duty because he already had an interest in photography. Luckily for Mama, his superiors gave him a weekend pass to spend some time with her. It was the last time she saw him alive.

I think the last true unspoiled moment of joy for Mama was about nine months after that Oklahoma City visit, when she gave birth to a healthy baby boy on July 2, 1945. She named me after the biblical figure, Isaac, because the name represented laughter and happiness to Isaac's mother.

I always wondered if Dad ever received word of my birth. He was in Okinawa at that point and Mama sent him a letter to let him know "she was now holding little Isaac." About a month after Mama sent that letter, Dad was dead.

On August 15, 1945, the Japan Broadcasting Corporation played a scratchy recording of Emperor Hirohito on the national airwaves. Hirohito had surrendered, and the war was over. Mama once told me about the moment she heard the surrender announcement on the radio. She said she was holding me and cried with so much joy that her tears fell into my eyes and set me off crying as well. Mama said she had to spend ten minutes swaying me back and forth to get me to stop bawling, but that didn't bother her at all. Mama's heart was full of joy. The war was over, and for the first time ever, we were going to be a complete family.

Three days later, Hideo Wakita snatched Mama's joy away and broke her heart into so many pieces that it could not be put back together.

My dad and the rest of his crew were flying over Tokyo in a B-32 Dominator. Their mission was to determine available routes for Allied forces to move into Tokyo and to review the status of several airfields nearby. Dad was the aerial photographer.

In the Japanese emperor's surrender message, he had asked his people to "beware most strictly of any outbursts of emotion which may engender needless complications." This bit of wisdom apparently did not connect with Wakita and two of his fellow pilots. When they spotted the B-32 flying over the skies of Tokyo, their rage got the better of them. They scrambled to their fighters to unleash that anger in an assault against the American plane.

The gunners aboard Dad's B-32 dispatched two of the three attackers without serious damage to the plane. But the remaining fighter pilot, Hideo Wakita, avoided the barrage of defensive fire. He opened fire on the plane with his 20mm cannon. One of the rounds ripped through the side of the plane and burst through Dad's chest. In my mind, I often pictured Wakita celebrating at the controls of his plane, peeling away from the murder scene of Eddie Wheeler, husband and first-time father. My father.

I never knew my dad, but I felt the bitterness of his loss every day of my life. Mama's grief was always like a lingering fog in our house. She took care of me and tried to provide a good home, but everything she did seemed somewhat mechanical. I rarely got her to talk because she was always busy with some household chore or outside smoking a cigarette. Sitting on the steps of Aunt Lois's house next door, Mama would smoke Old Gold cigarettes one right after another. I would watch the cigarette butts pile up at Mama's feet into little piles that reminded me of my Lincoln Logs.

My Aunt Lois was a war widow of a different kind. Her husband was Uncle Carl, my dad's brother, and although he returned from Europe alive, he brought back an amputated leg and a serious drinking problem. Uncle Carl died when I was about five years old, but Mama never told me what happened. I remember only a few small details about his funeral. His casket was closed. In my wide-eyed kid brain, I thought there was a skeleton inside the casket because I figured when you die, you instantly turn into a skeleton.

Then, one month after my fifteenth birthday, I discovered what death really looked like. I came home from school and found

Mama slumped over, sitting on the little bench next to the telephone. I remember looking at her feet, thinking there would be a pile of cigarettes there, like the murder weapon at the scene of the crime. Finding nothing there, I then looked at the phone to see if she had tried to pick it up and dial the operator, but the handset was still in the cradle. A thought flashed through my head that maybe she had felt something was wrong, that she had considered calling for help, and then she had chosen to just let go. I would always wonder, but I would never know. The official cause of death was a heart attack. But I have always known that Mrs. Lilly Wheeler truly died the moment Hideo Wakita murdered her husband in the skies over Tokyo after the war had already ended.

———

Aunt Lois said I would need to move in with her, and about a week after Mama's death, we began the process of going through Mama's things so the house could be put up for sale. After school one day, I went into Mama's room to go through the cedar chest she kept at the foot of her bed. She had the chest divided into partitions, and it looked like one side was for Mama's things and one side for my dad. On her side, I found an old pocket watch, a childhood doll, and some crocheted afghans. On Dad's side of the chest, the first item I picked up was a bag containing a sturdy little black and silver Argus brand camera. Along with the camera, there were two photographs in the bag. In one picture, Mama was leaning over a log fence and smiling so big I thought she must have been laughing when the picture was taken. The other photo showed Dad standing tall on the top fence rail with a proud smirk on his face. I imagined them holding the camera, taking the photos of each other, and just feeling so free.

I lingered on the pictures for a bit, and then I returned to the chest. There was a pistol lying there with "United States Property M1911 A1" marked on the side. Having never held a gun before, I lifted it out carefully. I can still remember feeling the weight of it in my hand. Just holding the gun made me feel like I had a different identity, like someone powerful.

Still clenching the gun in one hand, I reached into the chest to pick up a book which had a yellowed letter paperclipped to the front. In the letter, a Major General with the War Department had written to confirm a previous telegram that had been sent to notify Mama of Dad's death. The general went on to explain a few of the details surrounding the attack on Dad's plane, how they had valiantly fought off two of the three Japanese fighter planes, and that the United States had decided not to retaliate for the "post-surrender skirmish" in order to prevent continued loss of life. He concluded by mentioning that Dad's personal effects would be sent once they were received from his unit. Someone from Dad's unit must have slipped that gun in with the other items that were shipped to Mama.

That letter in Mama's cedar chest told me everything I ever knew about how Dad died, but the book she had attached the letter to told me who was responsible. The book was the 1958 autobiography of a famed Japanese fighter pilot named Hideo Wakita. With the help of an American co-author, Wakita had detailed his exploits during the war. Mama had marked a spot in the book with a folded sheet of paper. I set Dad's gun down on her bed and opened the book to the location Mama had saved. It was a chapter titled "One Final Shot." She had underlined most of it with a pencil.

In the chapter, Wakita described his final "combat mission" of World War II. He wrote of the shame he and his fellow pilots felt when they heard that their emperor had surrendered, and how that shame turned to rage when they saw an American bomber flying overhead. Wakita claimed he ran to his plane and the others followed to intercept the enemy. He went on to express regret for letting his emotions get the better of him, because his friends were shot down and he failed to take the enemy plane out of the sky.

There was no mention of my dad, but I knew from Mama's notes and the timeline that Hideo Wakita had fired the shot that took Dad's life. If Wakita had regrets about that little detail, he had not expressed them in his book. Mama had scratched through the word "enemy" anywhere it appeared in the chapter and written my dad's name above it.

I sat down on her bed with the book in my hands. My arms felt strange, like I had a hundred tiny pins poking me from underneath my skin. I could feel the intensity of Mama's anger, her sorrow, and her loneliness in every single one of those pencil strokes where she had crossed through "enemy" and replaced it with "Eddie." Feeling Mama's pain mixed with my own grief and hopelessness, pressure built in my chest like a balloon being inflated on my insides. My throat clogged, my face tensed up, and then it was as if the balloon burst inside of me. Tears erupted from my eyes with a force and suddenness that caught me by surprise. I wailed and I couldn't bring myself to a stop until, finally, my head started to pound, and I had a desperate need to catch my breath.

It took some time for me to compose myself. As I held my forehead in my hands, I noticed that the paper Mama had used to mark the chapter in Wakita's book had fallen to the floor. I picked it up and unfolded it to find a typed copy of the order of service for Dad's funeral. The service time, location, participants, and burial site were listed on the left-hand side. The date was three years after his death, because it had taken that long for his remains to be moved from the original burial site in Okinawa and relocated back home. On the right-hand side of the paper, "Sergeant Eddie Wheeler" was listed at the top and beneath his name was the phrase, "The last American combat death of the Second World War."

Mama had marked Wakita's "One Final Shot" chapter with that paper because it wasn't a plane, an anonymous soldier, or some faceless weapon of war that had killed her husband. It was Hideo Wakita, and the war was already over when he fired his one final shot.

I stuck Dad's pistol in my waistband and wrapped all the other items from Mama's cedar chest into one of the afghans. I pushed our creaky screen door open with my foot and began my slow march to Aunt Lois's house. With my arms full of all I had left of my family and my Dad's gun tucked away under my shirt, I thought about how great it would be if I could someday find Wakita and take one final shot of my own.

———

I MOVED into the upstairs bedroom of Aunt Lois's small one-and-a-half story house. She did everything she could think of to make me comfortable. We took the items I had collected from Mama's cedar chest and made a little memorial shelf on the wicker bookcase in Aunt Lois's kitchen. She told me that my Dad had bought the camera to take on the honeymoon when he and Mama got married. Dad had quickly fallen in love with photography and had an idea he might try to be a photographer for *Life* magazine.

Aunt Lois wasn't sure about the doll and the pocket watch from Mama's cedar chest, but she figured that it must have been Mama's doll and my grandpa's watch. Aunt Lois had no doubt that the baby blankets were mine, because she had made them. We lined the shelf with the blankets and arranged everything else on top.

But I kept Dad's gun and Wakita's book hidden under my

bed. Sometimes when I had trouble sleeping, I would turn on my lamp and just hold the gun while I read through Wakita's account of the day he murdered my Dad. I think subconsciously I thought I could somehow use the gun to change the outcome of that chapter as I read it, but the ending was always the same.

As the days and nights flowed by, the distractions of school and friends helped me to get moving again with my life. After Mama's death, I started to keep a journal of my thoughts and I discovered that I really enjoyed writing. That new interest in writing led me to join the school newspaper team.

In addition to the usual general interest articles I wrote, the editor allowed me to start a regular column called "The Pranks We Pull" in my senior year. Students would submit pranks they pulled on friends or relatives, and when we didn't get enough submissions, I would just fill in with jokes I had used on Mama or Aunt Lois in my younger years. My classmates loved the story of how I would cut out underwear model pictures from the Sears catalog and hide them in the hymnal where Aunt Lois or Mama sat at church. If I could get the church bulletin before they sat down, I would stash the pictures on the page for the hymn that we would be singing first that day. I'm pretty sure that prank got a few kids in trouble when they tried it out themselves. It was always worth it for the laughs, though.

That was the year I finally started to really feel like myself again after Mama's death. But graduation soon arrived, and the world came to test me again.

A lot of my friends headed off to college, but I had not given it much thought and I didn't have a way to pay for college anyway. One of the advisors for our school newspaper was Donald Hutcheson, who was also the editor for our city newspaper. Hutcheson was a First Lieutenant in the Marine Corps during World War II and I think he had taken an interest in me after he was told I lost my father in the war. He advised me to enlist in the US Marines. Things were uncertain in Vietnam at the time and if I enlisted instead of getting drafted later, my options would be better. He was an intelligent man and as close to a father figure as I had in my life, so I took his advice.

As I crossed the threshold into the recruiting office, Aunt Lois stood in the parking lot sobbing and pleading with me to reconsider. I hated to upset her, but I really didn't see any good alternative for me to pursue. Like most eighteen-year-olds, I was scared and macho and stupid all at the same time. I even had a thought that if I had to go to war, I might have an opportunity to rescue someone and prevent some kid from growing up without a dad. I was absolutely clueless.

I soon found out that there was no shortage of father figures available in the Marine Corps boot camp at Parris Island, South Carolina. They were called drill instructors and they were more than happy to give me guidance on where I should go, what I should do, when I should do it, and the general speed at which I should do it.

During boot camp, I questioned my sanity many times. I had volunteered to be tortured, and that should make any man stop and reflect a little on his choices. Somehow, to my surprise, I managed to make it through. The surprises continued when I found out that the United States Marine Corps had assigned me a military occupational specialty of 4312. I was going to be a journalist for the Marines.

I had no idea what qualified me for the job other than some typing skills, my time working on the school newspaper, and maybe something else they had seen from the various tests we were given. I had a suspicion that Mr. Hutcheson had somehow put in a word for me, but I never knew that for sure.

After boot camp, I had an opportunity to take some leave time, so I went home to see Aunt Lois. I'll never forget her reaction. She had been waiting on the steps where she and Mama used to have their chats. When she saw me coming down the sidewalk, Aunt Lois came running like an Olympic sprinter. She squeezed me so tight I thought I was going to have to explain how I got my ribs broken when I reported back from leave. I was trying to be a "tough Marine" and hold back the tears, but the strength of her happiness pressed on my heart. The tears came flowing out of me like a toddler with a skinned knee.

Over the course of my first few days at home, I'm not sure that she ever stopped talking. She wanted to know about what I had gone through, what kind of journalism training I was going to get, and where I'd be going after that. I'd answer as much as I could and then she would move on to some other topic. Aunt Lois shared just about every detail of town and church gossip she had heard, TV shows she had been watching, and books she had been reading. I got a little irritated with the never-ending chatter and after a week, I pondered an early return from leave.

Aunt Lois insisted I go with her to church the first Sunday I was home. After we got back from church, she made some lunch and we chatted a little more, of course. By the last spoonful of banana pudding, though, her eyes got a little droopy. A full belly and a lazy Sunday afternoon often have that effect on a person. I told her I would clean up and she disappeared into her room for the nap that was calling her name. As I sat in the kitchen, the quietness settled on my ears.

I walked over to the bookcase Aunt Lois kept in the kitchen to look at the memorial shelf we had made together. Mama's photo was propped up against her childhood doll, and Dad's picture lay against his old camera. I picked up the War Department letter that described Dad's final day on earth, wondering what outcome might lie ahead for me. It had been almost twenty years since he was murdered and five years since her heart stopped beating. I thought about what they might think of their son now. I wondered if they were walking happily together somewhere in heaven. Loneliness swept over me like it did when I first found all those items in Mama's cedar chest after she died.

I stood in Aunt Lois's silent kitchen thinking about myself, and then a thought flashed into my mind like a slap in the face. When she met me on the sidewalk the day I got home from boot camp, she wasn't just happy to see me and know that I was safe. Aunt Lois had been lonely too and she was elated to have someone she loved back in her life. I felt like a jerk. I had been focused on my situation and where I was going, and I hadn't given a thought to how alone she would be when I was gone.

With this newfound bit of good conscience, I dropped the selfish idea of returning early. Over the remaining days of my leave, I spent every minute I could with her. When time was growing short, I began to worry about how she would take care of herself while I was gone, forgetting she had managed just fine ever since Uncle Carl was first sent off to war. I envisioned myself in the John Wayne hero role and I decided she needed some protection while I wasn't around.

I slipped upstairs and then brought down the items I had kept stashed under my bed ever since Mama had died. Aunt Lois cried when I showed her Mama's notes in Wakita's book. But I think she gave serious consideration to bending me over her knee when she realized I had been hiding Dad's pistol all that time. The next day, I bought some ammunition and showed Aunt Lois how to load the magazine and chamber a round, but she wasn't interested in going out to a firing range to learn how to shoot. Even after I told her how I always wanted to take Wakita's book out and use it for target practice, she wouldn't change her mind. She put the gun and the book on the memorial shelf and told me it would be there when I got back.

When it was time for my leave to end, Aunt Lois became the "tough Marine" and kept it all together when we said goodbye. I swore to her that no matter where the Marines sent me, I would send her letters as much as possible. She told me not to worry about her, because I had plenty ahead to worry about. She was right. Things had escalated in Vietnam and after some additional training at Quantico, Virginia, I was on a plane to the other side of the world.

———

MY LAST STOPOVER before Vietnam was the island of Okinawa. The United States had kept control of Okinawa after the end of World War II and then used the island as a base for moving troops and equipment into and out of Vietnam. I had never been to Okinawa, but I knew before I arrived that I would despise the place. Nearly twenty years after my Dad had taken his final flight from the island, my boots were on the same cursed ground.

My time in Okinawa was like living a nightmare. I couldn't shake a nagging sense of dread and bizarre thoughts kept creeping into my mind. One awful night, I woke up with an overwhelming urge to go visit Dad's grave. It took a frightening amount of time to clear my head enough to remember that he was no longer buried on that horrible island.

My head just wasn't right the whole time I was there. The United States employed a multitude of Japanese citizens in various support roles on Okinawa. I would catch myself searching the faces of the men, hoping one of them might be Hideo Wakita. The idea was especially foolish because other than a tiny portrait of Wakita wearing a flight helmet in his book, I really had no idea what the man looked like. Undeterred, I daydreamed about what I might do if fate brought Wakita across my path. The feeling that I was somehow close to Wakita seemed to draw up anger that I had forgotten I had stored deep inside me. War or no war, I couldn't wait to get out of Okinawa and over to Vietnam. But then again, I was likely to be doing most of my fighting with a typewriter and not my rifle.

In the early fall of 1965, my time on Okinawa finally came to an end. I landed in Vietnam and began my work as a reporter for a new Marine newspaper called the *Sea Tiger*. The fact that I wasn't a combat Marine made it easier to keep my letter writing promise to Aunt Lois. I would send her minor details about articles I wrote for the paper, throwing in bits and pieces about interesting people that I had met. Aunt Lois would send me the latest town and church gossip, of course. I could tell she was always trying to be upbeat in her letters. The closest thing to a complaint I ever got from her was a comment she made about the hymnals not being as interesting since I left town.

Despite my nagging guilt about Aunt Lois, I felt like I had found a bit of purpose in my work for the *Sea Tiger*, so when the time came, I reenlisted. I visited Aunt Lois, using my reenlistment leave, and she talked nonstop like before, but this time she was sharing stories about what she had been up to with the group of ladies in her new garden club. She even brought me to a club meeting so she could "show me off" to all the ladies. My time with Aunt Lois flew by and near the end of my leave, a trace of sadness settled over the two of us. But things were different than they had been when I had last visited. I was still going to miss her, but I knew she wouldn't be lonely, and she knew I was doing something good with my life. Still, when I left, she hugged me so hard I thought she might crack one of my ribs. That woman was strong.

When I returned to Vietnam, my editor, Gunnery Sergeant Albert Banks, gave me an assignment to do a story on the Red Cross Supplemental Recreational Activities Overseas (SRAO) program. I had never heard of the program and I was more interested in combat correspondent work. I accepted the assignment without question, but I must not have hidden my disappointment very well. A smirk grew on his face as he told me that if I had a problem with the assignment, there were plenty of guys on staff who would love to interview one of the Donut Dollies. I hadn't heard of the SRAO, but I was quite familiar with the Dollies. I assured Gunny Banks that he could count on me and nothing would stop me from accomplishing my mission. Semper Fi.

The Donut Dollies were a group of women who had graduated from college, volunteered to come to Vietnam, and visited war zone facilities to help improve troop morale. The Dollies would host trivia games, play cards, talk with the guys, and just generally give the men a good reminder of home in a place that was nothing like it. They also served up refreshments, including millions of donuts during World War II, which led to the Donut Dollies nickname that everyone knew them by.

Two of these ladies were in Da Nang. I planned to first interview some Marine infantrymen in Da Nang so that I could get their thoughts on what the Dollies meant to them. Vietnam was as much of a hellhole to me as anyone, but these were the guys getting shot at. They had a much different war experience than I did. I wanted to get a better idea of how the Dollies lifted the spirits of the men who lived with the worst of Vietnam.

I walked into the Red Cross Center and found about half a dozen servicemen hanging out with two of the Donut Dollies who were wearing their signature light-blue dresses. One of the women was sitting with a group playing rummy and the other was chatting with a Marine who was strumming on a well-worn guitar. I wasn't about to interrupt any of the festivities at that moment, so I sat down and waited for an opportunity to do my interviews.

Both ladies were gorgeous and made a wonderful picture in a young Marine's eye, but the woman having the conversation with the guitar player grabbed my attention right away. I knew her job was to make the guys feel comfortable and relaxed, but she seemed to really be immersed in what he was saying. Sometimes the passion in people just radiates from their face without any effort.

She noticed me watching her and left the now unlucky Marine for a moment to find out if I needed anything. Her nametag had Grace printed on it and I quickly scribbled her name down at the top of my notepad, abandoning the notion of interviewing any of the fellows first.

I told her I was a reporter for the *Sea Tiger*, and I was there to make her famous. This got me the laugh I was looking for, but I blew my smooth intro when I froze up looking at her smile. It reminded me so much of the smile Mama had in that old photo, back when she was a joyful new bride leaning on a fence and unspoiled by the world. I wanted to just sit there soaking in the sunshine of her smile. The awkward silence got more awkward when guitar man stopped strumming and glared in our direction, looking to see who had stolen Grace from his private concert. I did my best to compose myself and get on with the interview.

I had blown my whole plan by not getting the perspective of the guys in combat to lead into my questions for her, so I stumbled at first. I decided to start with a hard-hitting question by asking her where she was from. I couldn't believe my luck when she told me she was from my own hometown. I think she thought I was making it up at first just to flirt with her, but she was familiar with the part of town where Aunt Lois and I lived.

Our conversation took off and if not for the competition from Corporal Rockstar and a couple other guys who had walked in, I think we could have talked for hours. I asked her why she had volunteered to come to Vietnam. She said that despite the chaos in the world, she felt like each person could make a positive difference through their own actions. For her, being a Donut Dollie at that time seemed like one of the best ways for her to do that.

Some people have a naïve optimism because they haven't really walked down some of life's darkest streets, but Grace had been in a war zone. Her eyes were wide open to the evils that people can do to one another. She felt that we each have an opportunity to do the right thing each time a choice comes before us, no matter how many times we've chosen the wrong thing before. It was way deeper than anything I was going to put into an article in the *Sea Tiger*, but she had me intrigued, to say the least.

I told her I'd have to wrap up the interview because if she kept all her attention on me, an Old-West-style saloon fight would break out any minute complete with guitars being smashed over heads. That got another hearty laugh out of her. Then I scrawled Aunt Lois's address and phone number onto a sheet in my notepad, tore it out, and told Grace to look me up whenever she got back home. I didn't know where I'd be, but I knew Aunt Lois would know. I figured guys were always making that offer to her and she was just humoring me, but it was fun to daydream about seeing Grace again someday.

Grace moved on to her next stop, and Aunt Lois and I continued to faithfully write each other. She sent me a note which included a photograph of her standing with the garden club ladies in front of her house. In her note, Aunt Lois said the photo was taken with my dad's old camera and she hoped I didn't mind. The girls wanted to get a picture after a recent meeting and that was the only camera in the house. I wrote back and told her the picture made me smile and she was welcome to anything I had there. I recommended she take the ladies on a field trip to the range with Dad's gun and shoot Wakita's book full of holes. After they were finished, she could mail it to me so

I could bury it in Okinawa the next time I passed through. She wrote back and told me that she didn't think the ladies would be interested in that field trip and that I should probably just bury that hate instead. That one stung just a bit.

I began to get more of the combat article assignments I was craving, and there were a few occasions when the old saying "be careful what you wish for" came to mind. Since I had basic training as a rifleman and I had already seen death in my life, I was stupid enough to think I was prepared for what I would see in the field. I quickly found out that death wounds your mind in many unexpected ways. The sights, sounds, and smells of humans killing other humans permanently changed the way I would sense and feel even the ordinary things in life. At the end of my second tour, I had never fired my rifle, but I was more than ready to head home.

———

THAT FIRST YEAR after leaving the Marines reminded me a lot of how I felt in the early days after Mama died. I really didn't know what to do with myself, but Aunt Lois was there to lift my spirits and drag me to church with her each Sunday. The Marines didn't provide me with a "how to rejoin society after living in a war zone" manual, so I just had to wing it. I did have the luxury of knowing someone who had managed the transition before, so I paid a visit to Donald Hutcheson, my old mentor and the man who recommended the Marines to me in the first place.

Hutcheson suggested that I take up a career as a freelance writer. Magazines and newspapers had a steady need for war-related stories, and I had a unique combination of writing skills and military experience which would help me get plenty of assignments. He made a few contacts for me and I was off and running.

Some of my old high school buddies began to come back home from college. We spent some time together, but it was like I was a zoo exhibit. They just wanted to ask me non-stop questions about things I had done or seen in Vietnam. In college, they had picked up a lot of anti-war political leanings and they wanted to spend time debating why we were in Vietnam. I just wanted to talk about anything but that place. Even when I was around friends, I still felt alone.

Relief arrived for me on August 2, 1969 in the form of a knock at Aunt Lois's door. I could not believe my eyes (in more ways than one) when I opened the door to see Grace Thompson, the Donut Dolly I had interviewed in Da Nang. I invited Grace in and led her to the kitchen so I could introduce her to Aunt Lois. Entering the kitchen, I was shocked to find Aunt Lois there with a mischievous grin on her face, a bowl of pretzels in her hands, and three bottles of RC Cola on the table. I raised an eyebrow and Aunt Lois confessed that Grace had called about a month earlier. Since then, the two of them had chatted on the phone a few times so that Grace could find out more about me. Aunt Lois had arranged for Grace to come by for a surprise visit. I told Aunt Lois I didn't want to hear any more comments about me being sneaky when I was hiding guns under my bed as a kid.

We sat around the kitchen table and shared stories for a few hours, talking about Grace's work with the Donut Dollies, my work on the *Sea Tiger*, and what we had been up to since we got back. I had to use my best journalistic skills to pry out the information Aunt Lois had been sharing on those secret phone calls with Grace. From what I could deduce, Aunt Lois had pretty much given Grace most of my life story up until Vietnam. Grace had still shown up on our doorstep after getting all those details, so I thought she must truly be interested in me. I knew Aunt Lois liked Grace too, or else there wouldn't have been pretzels and drinks at the ready when she arrived.

Grace and I began dating regularly and from the start we were just naturally comfortable together. She even knew the feeling of being alone when you were surrounded by friends who you couldn't really relate to. Grace was beautiful, intelligent, and so full of life. I had no doubt that she was the one for me. After six months of dating, I got down on one knee in Aunt Lois's kitchen and asked Grace to become Mrs. Isaac Wheeler. With Aunt Lois crying tears of joy and Mama and Dad smiling down from the shelf on Aunt Lois's bookcase, Grace Thompson said yes.

———

We weren't planning on any big to-do for the wedding, but Aunt Lois was hoping to at least have something her friends from the garden club could attend. We decided we would have a small ceremony in the chapel at her church.

On the night before our wedding, a few of my buddies wanted to take me out for a little bachelor celebration. I waited on Aunt Lois's steps for them to come and pick me up. Aunt Lois walked out and sat down beside me. She told me that many a marriage was ruined before they even got started by these little "wedding eve" parties. I assured her I would be on my best behavior and she told me she wasn't too sure she could trust the boy who planted underwear pictures in hymnals and kept a gun hidden under his bed. We laughed together and I reminded her that she wasn't allowed to accuse me of being sneaky any longer after her covert communications with Grace. Our chat came to an end when my friend pulled up in his electric blue Chevy Chevelle and honked the horn. As I walked away, I told her that I would conduct myself with the honor of a true US Marine.

Aunt Lois said that was exactly the thing that worried her, but she loved me either way. I just blurted out "thanks" as I hopped in the car.

I was true to my word that night. We primarily shot pool, drank beer, and swapped stories. Some of the stories may have been true, but most were probably not. A lot of twenty-five-year-olds would have tried to make the night a bit wilder, but I had packed in a lot more than twenty-five years' worth of living in my time. I was very happy just hanging out and relaxing.

We called it a night relatively early and got back to the house just after 11 p.m. I walked up the sidewalk with thoughts of new beginnings on my mind. Then I noticed that someone was lying across the steps. I felt like I was ripping apart on the insides as my heart refused to agree with what my mind had recognized.

There are moments in the story of your life that make you want to close the book before you finish. As I held Aunt Lois's lifeless body in my arms in the spot where I had left her just a few hours earlier, her story was finished, and I had no desire to add any new chapters to my own.

I drifted through the next couple of days in an almost dream-like state. I felt numb, like I was watching everything unfold in front of me, but I wasn't really there. It seemed surreal, and I even found myself wondering whether it was me who was truly dead. Maybe I was somehow seeing things from the other side. Flowers had been delivered to the house, meant for our wedding but now symbols of mourning.

Grace had been by my side as soon she had received word. I told her I felt like I had been given more than my fair share of tragedy. I wondered if something evil was out to get me by taking the women in my life. Grace tried to comfort me and reminded me that we still had each other, and nothing was going to take her away. I don't know that I believed her.

The world immediately felt different for both of us. All our future plans had involved Aunt Lois. Grace and I had purchased a home just down the street so we could be close to her, and I had expected to take care of Aunt Lois well into old age. Instead, a stroke had taken her at only fifty-eight years old on the night before our wedding was supposed to take place. We buried Aunt Lois three days later in the church cemetery next to Uncle Carl.

After the graveside service, I walked Grace over to the spot where Mama and Dad were buried. Dad's tombstone had the same inscription that was printed in his funeral program, "The last American combat death of the Second World War." Grace wanted to know the story behind that, because it hadn't come up in her talks with Aunt Lois. She had only told Grace that Dad was killed in World War II, Mama died when I was fifteen, and that she had been taking care of me ever since.

I told Grace the story of Dad's final day, how Mama had been affected by it, and how in a way, Hideo Wakita's choice to shoot after the war was over had ultimately led me to that moment. I was standing in the cemetery with all the people I loved gone except for Grace. She reminded me of the words that she had shared with me back in Vietnam. How we each have an opportunity to do the right thing each time a choice comes before us, no matter what has happened leading up to that choice. Grace said the right thing for us to choose now was to let time bring healing and to move forward with our lives. I wasn't sure if I had the energy to do that.

———

TWO WEEKS after Aunt Lois had passed away, I stepped back into her house for the first time. I had told Grace that I was just going to pack some of my own things to move into our new house. I had no desire to torment myself by going through Aunt

Lois's stuff. I would need Grace to take care of that for me someday, but I wasn't planning on it anytime soon.

I went upstairs to my room and brought down a black duffel bag so that I could pack up the memory shelf Aunt Lois and I had made together. The kitchen was silent except for the ticking of the clock on the stove and the occasional creaking of the floor as I walked. Aunt Lois had kept everything arranged on the shelf just as it was when I had left for Vietnam. The only change was the picture of her with her garden club which I had added to the shelf when I returned home. I packed it into the bag with the pictures of Mama and Dad. All happy faces that I would never see again in this life.

Pulling the magazine out from Dad's gun, I eased the slide back to check for a round in the chamber. I figured Aunt Lois would have unloaded the gun at some point, but apparently, she had never once touched it. I replaced the magazine and set the gun in the bag.

I picked up Wakita's book and began to open it to the "One Final Shot" chapter like I always did. But as I went to that page that Mama had marked with Dad's funeral program, Aunt Lois's letter to me in Vietnam drifted into my mind. The letter where she told me to bury my hate for Wakita in Okinawa. I sat listening to the steady click from the stove clock and nothing else but the thoughts in my head. Hoping to feel some kind of comfort, something other than grief, I pulled Mama's bookmark out and tossed Wakita's book into the trash can. If that was supposed to make me feel better, it didn't work. The silence in the house was getting to me, so I finished putting the rest of the items from the shelf into my duffel bag, zipped it closed, and headed for the front door.

As I walked outside, I was startled to hear Aunt Lois's phone ring. I set the bag down on the steps and ran back inside to answer. On the line was Paul MacMillan, one of the editors for

Reader's Monthly magazine. I had done a few freelance articles for the front section of the magazine and Paul liked my writing and he liked working with me.

MacMillan was a Korean War veteran and he told me that he had recently met a man at an American Legion meeting with an interesting story. The man was a World War II veteran and his son had married a Japanese woman. This wasn't that intriguing by itself, but the woman's father had fought for the Japanese during the war, and her father had recently moved to the United States to live with his daughter and son-in-law due to health reasons. MacMillan said the long, controversial war in Vietnam had created a public thirst for stories of reconciliation and forgiveness. He thought the premise for this story would be how the two fathers-in-law were making things work, putting away old grievances for the good of the family.

MacMillan thought the story would be a good fit for me. I could relate to the two veterans because of my own experience, and I had a connection to World War II because my dad had served. I was only about a two-hour drive from where the family lived, and it was a chance to get a feature article in *Reader's Monthly*.

The story sounded interesting and even if it hadn't, I would have probably taken it just to get my mind off everything else. I told him I would take the assignment and he said he would mail me the contract with the terms for the article. I asked him if he had an address or phone number for the family so I could get a head start. MacMillan gave me the name, address, and phone number for the daughter and then the names of the two fathers-in-law.

I don't know if I said anything else after that. The next thing I recall was sitting down at Aunt Lois's kitchen table and staring at the last thing I had written on her notepad. The name of the father-in-law who had fought for the Japanese in World War II was Hideo Wakita.

At first, I thought I might have written it wrong since I had just been looking at Wakita's book. I called MacMillan back and he said we had been disconnected somehow, but yes, that was the name of the man who fought for the Japanese that I was going to interview. MacMillan said he thought the man had been a fighter pilot, but he wasn't certain about that detail. I thanked him and hung up the phone properly.

A thousand different thoughts raced through my mind as I walked back outside. My head ached and one of my ears was ringing, so I sat down on the step next to my duffel bag. I felt like someone had just added one plate too many on a tall stack of dishes and everything was about to crash to the ground. Sitting there, I ran through so many scenarios of what this meant and how I was supposed to deal with it. As the day slipped toward twilight, I looked down at my bag which was lying in almost the same spot where I had found Aunt Lois. The last time I had sat there, she had told me she loved me no matter what I did and like an idiot, I had simply said, "Thanks." My jaw tensed and then an idea floated into my consciousness like an autumn maple leaf gliding to the ground. Sometimes thoughts appear in your mind so clearly it makes you feel like someone else had to put them there.

I went back into the house, retrieved Wakita's book from the trash, and dropped it into to the bag with the rest of my memories. Either God or the devil had delivered Hideo Wakita to me, and I was going to have Wakita take one more shot.

———

THE NEXT DAY, Grace and I got together for lunch and I told her that I was taking on a new assignment to get my mind onto something else. Before I could finish telling her about it, she got up from her seat and hugged me so tight it rivaled one of Aunt Lois's goodbye hugs. Grace had been worried about my mental state and she loved the idea of me getting back to work.

I explained the general notion behind the story and Grace's smile just kept expanding as I went over *most* of the details. I felt bad about not telling her Wakita was involved. But I knew if I told her, she would try to stop me. I asked her to come along with me on the interview and she was thrilled. Grace was a crucial part of what I had planned, although she didn't know it yet.

One week later, Grace and I were on the road. I kept the radio on for most of our trip so that I could organize my thoughts. She had her nose buried in a new book, so she had no complaints. I can't remember much about the two hours I spent driving on that highway, but I'll never forget listening to "Fire and Rain" by James Taylor as I parked in front of the home of Hideo Wakita.

Grace gave me a curious look when she saw me grab my black duffel bag from the back seat, but I guess she just thought it had my materials for the interview and she didn't ask me about it. I wasn't sure what I would say if she had.

After a ring of the doorbell, I had a small sense of relief when Wakita's daughter was the person who opened the door. She had shoulder-length jet-black hair and her eyes sparkled a little in the morning sunlight. She was holding a baby who looked like she couldn't be more than three months old or so. I told her we were there to interview the family for the *Reader's Monthly* article, and she invited us in.

The living room was long and somewhat narrow. A pair of couches, bright as sunflowers, sat opposite each other with a coffee table in the middle. Wakita's daughter, Emiko, introduced us to her father-in-law, who had been sitting in one of two leaf-patterned chairs at the far end of the room. He was wearing a t-shirt with "Property of US Army" printed across the front. I wondered if he wore it for this occasion or if he always put it on just to antagonize Wakita.

Emiko offered one of the couches for Grace and me to sit. She called out to her husband to let him know the reporters had arrived. Setting my duffel bag down on the floor by the coffee table, I felt a lump forming in my throat.

Emiko's husband came into the room, and we all introduced ourselves. Passing the baby to her husband as he settled into the chair next to his dad, Emiko excused herself so she could go get "Chichi" while the rest of us made small talk.

Grace was doing a great job leading the chitchat and I had tuned it all out. I was wrapped up in my thoughts, telling myself to "complete the mission" and "stay on point" over and over again. As Grace spoke, I was nodding at what I hoped were the right times, because I had no idea what was being discussed. I was trying to strengthen my resolve.

The noise in my head went instantly silent when the man entered the room, followed by his daughter. He looked to be around sixty years old, small in stature and sicklier than he should have for his age. He walked with the aid of a cane. Emiko helped her father to sit in the couch across from us and introduced him to me and Grace.

For a moment, I felt like I was watching the scene unfold from somewhere behind my eye sockets. I was in the living room of Hideo Wakita, and he was sitting directly across from me. I closed my eyes and I was fifteen again, staring at Mama slumped over next to the telephone. I drew in a deep breath, opened my eyes, and fixed my gaze on the man who had killed my parents.

I told him my name was Isaac Wheeler, and I asked him if he was familiar with the name Wheeler. Emiko told me her father's

English was not great and that she would translate when she needed to. She repeated my question to Wakita, and he shook his head and told her no, but he didn't read *Reader's Monthly* so he would not have seen my articles.

I responded by saying I wasn't the Wheeler I was asking him about. I unzipped the duffel bag and Grace gave me a strange look I had never seen from her before. I took Wakita's book out, tapped the cover, and asked if it was him. He nodded and his daughter answered without translating the question. It was his book.

Grace put her hand on my leg and gripped hard enough to cause me some pain. She could see that I had packed everything from my memory shelf into the duffel bag. I set his book on the coffee table and pressed on.

I pulled out the photos of Mama and Dad. I told him who they were, how the photos were taken not long after they were married, and that my father had later gone to fight in the Second World War. Emiko continued to cheerily translate all of this.

I laid the photos on the table and then I pulled out the sheet with Dad's funeral program printed on it. I told Wakita that my dad was killed in the war, and I read the text under Dad's name on the program aloud.

"The last American combat death of the Second World War."

This piqued the interest of Emiko's father-in-law, who asked to see the funeral program. Grace handed it to him while Emiko translated what I had said to Wakita. He nodded and waited for me to continue with the conversation.

I opened Wakita's book to the "One Final Shot" chapter. In that moment, I was overwhelmed with sorrow, seeing all Mama's pencil marks where she had written Dad's name and knowing I was in the presence of the man who had caused all her pain. I leaned over the table with the open book gripped firmly in my left hand. With my right hand, I snatched Dad's picture off the coffee table held it next to the book for Wakita to see. Then, like the Hoover Dam bursting, I unleashed a verbal fury in that living room. Thrusting Dad's photo toward Wakita, I told him that he was the man who killed my dad after the war was over and I had hated him for murdering my father like a shadowy thug in the alleys of the Tokyo sky. He had ruined Mama's life, and I told him how I had discovered his book in her things after I found Mama dead. Brandishing the book at Wakita, I explained how she had marked through his word for enemy and written my Dad's name in its place. Like a judge chastising the defendant before handing down his sentence, I was unloading my emotions, and I felt like I was unloading all of Mama's hurt on Wakita for her.

Emiko had stopped translating at some point and I have no idea how much Wakita had understood. Now sobbing, Emiko's face was sadness and fear all scrambled together. Grace had a hold of the back of my shirt like she thought I was going to leap across the table.

Emiko's husband stood up and demanded that I leave, pointing toward the door. Wakita held up a hand for him to stop and at the same time, I removed Dad's pistol from the bag and rested it on the table. I don't know if it was Wakita's hand or the gun, but the desired effect was achieved. His son-in-law backed away.

The baby was crying, and Emiko took her from her husband. Wakita motioned for his son-in-law to sit and said something in Japanese, all the while keeping his eyes locked with mine. The thought crossed my mind that this man was a soldier all the way to the end.

Emiko was swaying the baby to comfort her, and the room fell silent except for the soft squeak of the baby's pacifier. I told Emiko there was more to tell, and I asked if we could continue.

She glanced at Grace, who gave a slight nod, and then Emiko said I could finish what I had to say.

I told Wakita the story of how I had found Dad's gun after Mama's death. Then I described how I used to hold the gun and daydream about killing him with it. After Emiko translated this, Wakita knew enough English to reply for himself this time.

"I would have done the same."

Grace still had the back of my shirt in her fist, but she loosened her grasp when I turned to Emiko and apologized for the chaos I had brought to her home. I went on to tell them all a little about Aunt Lois, what she meant to me, and how I had lost her just a few weeks earlier. Then I explained the phone call from *Reader's Monthly* which had brought me to their house. Finally, I revealed that I had come there to bury my hate, as Aunt Lois had once advised, and I wanted Hideo Wakita to help me.

I asked Emiko if she would ask her father to stand. Her husband began to protest but she translated my request anyway. Wakita reached for his cane and pulled himself up.

I looked at Grace and I told her I was sorry for not sharing my plan with her. I was afraid she wouldn't go along, and this was something I felt I had to do. I grabbed the last item I was going to take from the bag, and Grace smiled at me when she realized what I was up to. I took her hand and we stood together. I was holding Dad's camera.

Emiko gave the baby back to her husband and stood next to her father to translate and help steady him. I explained that the camera was my Dad's and how he had hoped to be a photographer someday. The camera had always represented good times for my family. The pictures I had shown them of Mama and Dad were taken with it, and I described the happy garden club picture Aunt Lois had sent me in Vietnam.

I told Wakita I had been to war and I understood what it could do to a man. I didn't know if I would have made the same choices he did on August 18, 1945. All I could control were the decisions I had to make in the present. I looked Hideo Wakita straight in the eye, and I told him that I forgave him for what he did that day.

Grace was crying as Emiko finished translating for her father. Wakita began to say something but I held out the camera and interrupted him. I knew it was a strange request, but I wanted to know if he would be willing to take a picture of Grace and me together.

He took the camera from me and I wrapped my arm around Grace's waist and pulled her close. She had time to dry her eyes while Emiko gave her father a few instructions on how to operate the camera. I smiled big, imagining what Aunt Lois would think about this scene as Hideo Wakita pressed the shutter release on Dad's camera to take a picture of me and Grace.

———

SINCE I WANTED to start writing about everything that had just happened while it was fresh on my mind, I asked Grace to drive home. She drove but there was very little writing. Grace gave me multiple pieces of her mind for not telling her about Wakita before our trip. I took my medicine and made no defense. She seemed like she was running out of steam when we were close to home, so I flipped the radio on when there was a moment of silence. I was hoping to distract her from getting a second wind.

As we pulled into the carport of our newly purchased home, the song "All Right Now" was blasting through our speakers. I had to agree with the radio gods on that one.

Over the next couple of weeks, I did my best to write a short story of my life and all the unbelievable things that had transpired with Hideo Wakita. I dropped my article into a mailing envelope and typed up a note for Paul MacMillan, my editor at *Reader's Monthly*. In the letter, I acknowledged that I hadn't written exactly what we had talked about, but it was a good fit for his war reconciliation and forgiveness piece. I thought his readers might find the story I wrote a little more interesting than the original concept. If he decided to publish it, I insisted he keep the caption and credit for the included photo just as I had written it.

Grace and I rode to the post office together to send off the story. As I steered into the parking lot, I told her I probably wouldn't ever use Dad's camera again. Raising an eyebrow, she shrugged her shoulders and told me she didn't see any problem with that. I grinned and dropped the story into the outgoing mail slot.

Months later, Grace and I were officially husband and wife and enjoying life in our new home. On the day a copy of *Reader's Monthly* arrived in the mail, I nearly crashed into Aunt Lois's old bookshelf as I rushed into our house to look at the magazine with Grace. My story had been published and MacMillan had honored my request to keep the caption just as I had written it. There in the middle of *Reader's Monthly* magazine, was a picture of Grace and me standing in front of a sunflower-yellow couch, and printed underneath was "One Final Shot – Taken by Hideo Wakita."

HISTORICAL NOTE

This story is a work of historical fiction inspired by an actual event. Sergeant Anthony Marchione of Pottstown, Pennsylvania was the last American to die in combat in World War II. Sergeant Marchione was a gunner and photographer's assistant aboard a B-32 which was attacked by Japanese fighter pilots three days after Japan had surrendered. He was survived by his parents and two sisters. His sacrifice and bravery, along with many, many others, has enabled all Americans to live in the land of the free.

Lost at Thaxton: The Dramatic True Story of Virginia's Forgotten Train Wreck

A record storm triggers a deadly train wreck. As 18 perish in the burning debris, survivors fight for life in this thoroughly researched true story of the 1889 disaster, written by the great-great grandson of the railroad section master at Thaxton.

Copper and the Tree Frog: The Night Heron Nabbing

Join Copper the house cat and her friends as they solve the mystery of the disappearing night herons in this educational and laugh out loud novel for ages 8 to 12.

ABOUT THE AUTHOR

Michael Jones was planted in West Virginia and cultivated in South Carolina, with roots extended deep into Virginia soil. He loves writing fiction, non-fiction, and children's books. For his children's books, he writes under the super-creative pen name, Mike Jones. You can find out more about Michael and sign up to be notified about new releases at mikejoneswrites.com.

ACKNOWLEDGMENTS

A huge thanks goes to my beta readers, Robyn Roberson, Gene and Peggy Jones (aka Mom and Dad), and Todd McDonald, who all gave their time to read, critique, and improve *One Final Shot*. An extra-special shout-out goes to Dr. Laura Rotta, who not only read *One Final Shot*, but also applied her superhuman editorial skills to help me get the words right. Any issues that remained in the story were a result of revisions I foolishly made without consulting that grammatical guru.

As always, my greatest gratitude goes to my family, Monica, Mason, and Molly, who make me the luckiest husband and father on earth, and my Lord, Jesus Christ, who died on the cross to give us all a chance to be lucky children of God.